Sam

Amelia

David

Timothy

Robert

Amanda

Belinda

Moss

Marcus

For Claire and Lucy

N. M.

For Gillian

A. A.

First published in the United States 1995 by
Dial Books for Young Readers
A Division of Penguin Books USA Inc.
375 Hudson Street
New York, New York 10014

Published in Great Britain by Orchard Books
Text copyright © 1994 Nicola Moon
Pictures copyright © 1994 by Alex Ayliffe
Printed in Belgium
First Edition
1 3 5 7 9 10 8 6 4 2

Library of Congress Cataloging in Publication Data
Moon, Nicola.
Lucy's picture / by Nicola Moon
pictures by Alex Ayliffe.
p.   cm.
Summary: A young girl creates a special picture that her blind
grandfather can "see" with his hands.
ISBN 0-8037-1833-0
[1. Grandfathers—Fiction. 2. Blind—Fiction. 3. Physically
handicapped—Fiction. 4. Art—Fiction.]
I. Ayliffe, Alex, ill. II. Title.
PZ7.M776Lu   1995   [E]—dc20   94-11178   CIP   AC

The artwork was produced as collage.

Lucy's Picture

Nicola Moon

pictures by Alex Ayliffe

Dial Books for Young Readers

NEW YORK

"My grandpa's coming to visit today," said Lucy. "How nice," said Mrs. Kelly. "Now, take a seat because we're all going to do some painting."

"Can I do a picture for Grandpa?" asked Lucy.

"Of course you *may*," said Mrs. Kelly.

Lucy looked at the big sheet of white paper in front of her.

"Can't you think of what to paint, Lucy?" asked Mrs. Kelly.

"What would your grandpa like? Something nice and bright? Look at those lovely colors!"

Lucy looked at the red and the yellow and the sky-blue paints. "They're not right," she said. "May I use the glue? May I stick things on to make a picture?"

"You mean a collage? Of course! But you'll have to sit at another table. There's not enough room here."

Lucy took her paper to an empty table in the corner. She went and found a bottle of glue, some scissors, and the box of scraps.

Lucy loved Mrs. Kelly's box of scraps. She liked plunging her hands deep in the box and feeling with her eyes shut.

Lucy started her picture. She cut some soft green velvet into curvy mounds for hills, and stuck them on the paper. She made a lake out of blue shiny stuff, and put it in between the hills.

Then she found some flowery dress material.

"Grandpa has flowers like this in his garden," Lucy told Mrs. Kelly. Lucy cut around the flowers and stuck them in little clumps along the edge of the lake.

At recess Lucy was too busy to play. Instead she
collected twigs, leaves, and two small feathers. Then
she filled her empty juice cup
with sand from the sandbox.
At last it was time to go inside.

Scrapbox

Now Lucy was even more excited about Grandpa's picture. She made him a tree out of the twigs and the leaves, and stuck the feathers on the end of a branch. Then she squeezed a long winding ribbon of glue over the hills, and sprinkled sand over the glue to make a path.

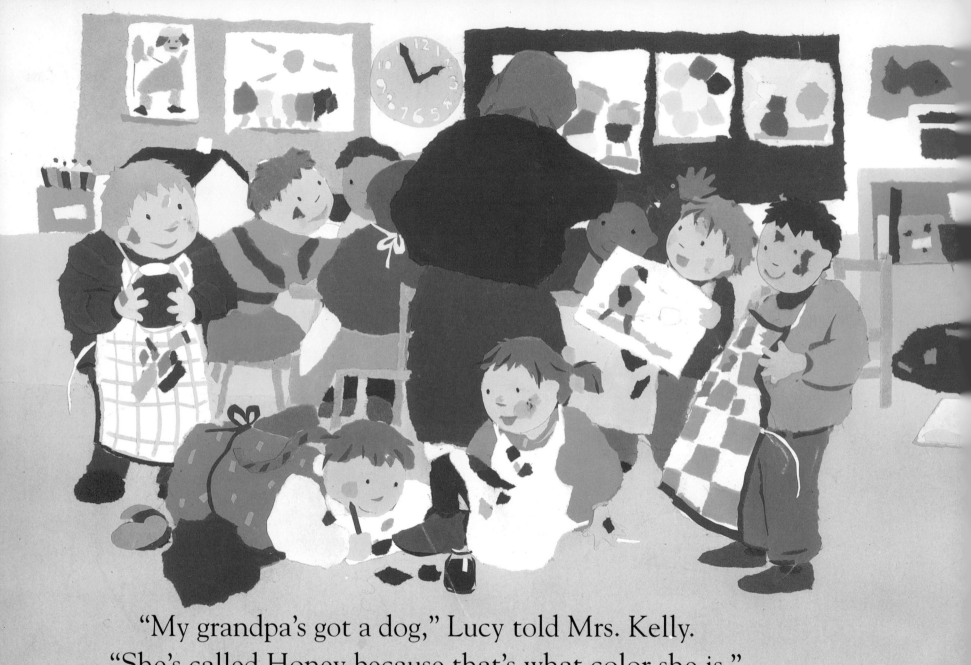

"My grandpa's got a dog," Lucy told Mrs. Kelly.
"She's called Honey because that's what color she is."
When Mrs. Kelly wasn't looking, Lucy trimmed
a piece of her own hair and glued it to a dog she had
made from a piece of paper.

Scrapbox

"That's lovely, Lucy," said Mrs. Kelly when it was storytime. She put Lucy's picture safely on the side to dry along with all the paintings.

Lucy couldn't wait to go home. She hadn't seen Grandpa in a long time.

Her mother was waiting as usual, but today there
was someone with her.
"Grandpa!" cried Lucy. She nearly knocked him off his feet.

"I made you a picture, Grandpa. Look. . . ." Lucy grabbed her blind grandfather's hand and guided it over her picture. "These are hills, and here's the road. . . ."

Grandpa touched the picture carefully. "A tree. A bird. And what's this? It feels like your hair, Lucy."

"That's Honey!" said Lucy, smiling.

"How clever! And what a wonderful surprise. It's the best picture I've ever seen," said Grandpa.

Lucy

And hand in hand, Grandpa and Lucy and her mother walked home.

Sara

Gillion

William

Katie

Sally

Daisy

Henry

Jonathan